THE HARP

THE HARP

by

Monica Lövström

Based on a true story

Thank you
Anna Holmén
for living an inspiring life

and
Hugh Dow
for linguistic – and moral – support

Anna had just poured a cup of tea when the doorbell rang. She opened the door cautiously, the area where she lived demanded that, and she spotted a huge harp in a pink cover. She was startled. It was not common to find harps outside your home in this area. In fact, she was fairly certain it didn't happen regularly in any part of the Town.

Then a very small girl with long, delicate fingers peeped out from behind the very pink and very big harp.

"Excuse me ma'am, could you be so kind as to look after my harp overnight?"

Anna must have looked very startled because the girl hurriedly continued:

"I'm supposed to give a concert in the community hall here" – she waved vaguely in direction of the other side of the street – "and wanted to put my harp there, to give it a little time to settle in. But the hall was locked."

The girl sighed. Anna quickly ran a couple of scenarios in her head, calculating the probability that the instrument was part of some criminal master plan. Then she nodded.

"Of course. For the sake of the harp. It wouldn't be safe in many of the houses around here." She felt sure that it would be sold on the black market the second after her neighbour got his hand on it, for example. And she had already warmed to the bulky and cumbersome instrument that looked so heart-breakingly out of place in the melting snow on the pavement.

Anna took a step down to give the Girl a hand, but the tiny creature lifted it up herself and wheeled it through the hallway.

"So, there", said the Girl with a certain finality in her voice. "Thank you, ma'am. I'll be back tomorrow afternoon." She patted the bulkier side of the Harp as you would pat a horse, and the instrument responded with low thuds.

The rest of the evening Anna spent catching up on Game of Thrones and when she went to bed, she had all but forgotten about her new boarder downstairs.

In the morning, barely awake, Anna jumped at the sight of the Harp but then her memory began to come back slowly and unwillingly. She decided that the Harp was in her way – indeed, she would have to squeeze herself between the dining table and the instrument to get to the kettle, and the kettle was like a life support system to her in the mornings. Without black builder's tea to kick start her brain, she felt weak.

Anna tried to shift the Harp. It wouldn't budge. She tried a little harder. Even when she clenched her teeth, she only managed to tilt it a little. But surely the small girl with delicate fingers had moved it herself? Anna decided it was time for a cup of tea and squeeeezed herself into the kitchen.

Five minutes later she stood looking at the Harp with mug in hand. Sipping the tea, she got curious about how to play such a weird and beautiful instrument. She put her cup at the kitchen counter and carefully removed the cover.

She plucked a string – doing – and another – doing, doiiing – the sound reverberated through the house, in a beautiful and elvish way. But then she stopped. She oughtn't. It wasn't hers to play. She was its guardian.

The afternoon came, but no girl with delicate fingers. Actually, no girl at all. Only Anna's husband. He arrived towards the evening after having spent three weeks at sea and was pleased to see the instrument.

"Have you taken up music?" he asked with a big grin. "Are you going to quit work?"

Anna sighed and explained, finishing with: "If the Girl doesn't come tomorrow, I'll call someone to come and pick it up. It's in the way."

The next day, she circled around the Harp, well tried to as best as she could in the tiny room. As she did so she saw a little metal plaque on its base. Anna got down on her hands and knees and tried to read what it said: "Te-lyn hud", she spelled out slowly. Telyn hud? What could that mean? Was it the maker's name? She pondered over it for a while, but then she started to wonder what it would feel like to play it and plucked a couple of strings again. Doiing. Doiiing... And why were some of the strings blue? And some red? She picked up her tablet and searched YouTube for videos on how to play the harp. She felt utterly silly, knowing fully well that it takes years to learn how to play an instrument.

"But since it is sitting here in my living room, I might as well see what it feels like. If the Girl doesn't come and pick it up by the weekend, I'll call for someone to help us get rid of it."

"I will!!" she added, looking at her husband, who

just smiled and nodded.

"Of course", he answered, "that's the wisest thing to do."

But right now, the most important thing was to get the Harp out of the doorway to the kitchen. It would be terribly difficult to cook and eat dinner with that thing in the middle of everything. They couldn't order pizza again tonight. During her research on the internet Anna found that she must tilt the Harp away from her to be able to move it on its tiny wheels. Very carefully she manoeuvred the Harp further into the living room.

Then she spent most of the coming week with the Harp. Touching the strings, thudding the bulky part, which she learned was called a "soundbox".

A couple of days later there were people at the door again. "The Girl!" Anna thought, but this time it was three youngsters, with a wide array of musical instruments sticking out from their cases and backpacks, that have rung her bell.

"So, they've finally come to pick up the Harp", Anna thought and felt a sadness growing inside her. She didn't understand why, she shouldn't be sad to get that huge thing out of their tiny house.

To her utter astonishment, the youngsters asked her to play at the Christmas concert on the other side of the street. The original one had been cancelled due to the disappearance of one of the soloists – the harp player. It took a couple of seconds, but then she burst out laughing. She had to admit that this was one of the most elaborate practical jokes she'd ever heard of! But it was actually not a very good one. Not by any standards!

Looking a bit perplexed, the young man handed over some sheet music.

"But I can't play the harp! And I can certainly not read music!" Anna said, still chuckling.

"At the music school they said that you could", he answered with a shrug of that kind which young people master to perfection, and then the three of them turned around and walked away.

Anna watched them walk away through the heavy snowfall and didn't know what to do. She returned to her living room and looked at the papers in her hand. "The First Noël" it said. Great! At least she recognised the name of the song. That's always something, she thought with a sigh. She looked up the particular piece of music on YouTube. She listened. It was a short piece, so she listened again. And again. It was so beautiful!

Then Anna sat down at the Harp, adjusting herself on the stool, clenched and opened her fists a couple of times, and cleared her throat. She still felt silly, but figured that this was something musicians did when they sat down with their instrument. Then she started to play. She just knew how to move her fingers and hands, what pedals to move. She played the piece! "What kind of magic is this?!" went through a part of her brain, the more rational part, which was slow to react since she seemed to have left it on the bathroom shelf this morning. Ok, her fingers were sore, her shoulder ached terribly, her head was buzzing, but she could. actually. play!

In good time for the concert, the three young musicians arrived again without their instruments sticking out from their backpacks, but with a small trolley. "So this is goodbye", Anna thought when they packed the Harp in its cover, tipped it on to the trolley and walked away. She followed them to the door and watched them wheel the Harp down the street, making a trail in the snow, and she was suddenly overcome by sadness.

She took a couple of hesitant steps after them, and then started to run. Anna, the Harp and the three musicians entered the Community Hall together and there she sat down to watch them set up the instruments, the stools and music stands for the concert. Some were busy decorating the stage with holly and sparkling stars. Part of her felt a fluttering excitement, part of her thought that all of this was utter nonsense.

But Anna bravely took the stage when it was her turn to play. She heard the song in her head and managed to channel the sound out into her fingers which moved a bit clumsily over the strings, but still didn't play many false notes. Just a couple.

After her final note, Anna got standing ovations from the audience. All 32 of them! She still couldn't really believe what had happened but decided not to dwell on it and just ride the tidal wave of happiness she felt.

When she finally went back stage Anna saw the small Girl with delicate fingers sneak away with a big smile on her face. Who knows, perhaps it was a trick of the light back there, but later Anna would swear the Girl had tiny angel's wings.

www.ingramcontent.com/pod-product-compliance
Lightning Source LLC
Chambersburg PA
CBHW020258180726
47994CB00028B/3171